S0-BOA-313

Tumbler

For Gabriel Filleul L.F.
For Helen Paterson S.F.

Text copyright © 2001 Liz Filleul
Illustrations copyright © 2001 Susan Field
This edition copyright © 2001 Lion Publishing

The moral rights of the author and illustrator have been asserted

Except for brief quotations in critical articles or reviews, no part of this book may be reproduced in any manner without prior written permission from the publisher. Write to: Permissions, Augsburg Fortress, Box 1209, Minneapolis, MN 55440.

First Augsburg Books edition. Originally published as *Tumbler* copyright © 2001 Lion Publishing plc., Sandy Lane West, Oxford, England

ISBN 0-8066-4268-8
AF 9-4268

First edition 2001

01 02 03 04 05 1 2 3 4 5 6 7 8 9 10

Printed in Malaysia

Tumbler

Liz Filleul

Illustrated by Susan Field

Augsburg Books
Bringing Families Together
For Children & Families

Tristan was a member of a troupe of minstrels.
People loved to watch Tristan's acrobatics.
Afterward all the children would spend hours
practicing cartwheels and handstands, wanting to
be like Tristan when they grew up.

Although Tristan had been a tumbler since he was a very young boy, his greatest wish was to serve God. During his travels, he had often seen monks helping the poor and feeding the hungry. He thought their work was much more special than his.

Tristan didn't tell any of the other minstrels about his ambition because he thought they would laugh at him. But he said his prayers every night, promising God that one day he would be one of those monks, giving food to the poor.

One day the troupe was performing on a village green. The villagers applauded, looking forward to the acrobatics to come.

As usual, Tristan turned cartwheels and somersaulted, leaping high in the air. But at the end of one jump he tripped and stumbled. He stood up and limped away, unable to finish his tumbling routine.

Later, the other minstrels sat down on the grass beside Tristan and looked at his leg.

"That's going to take a while to heal," commented Felix the storyteller. "You need to take a rest."

Felix was right, Tristan decided. It was time to give up tumbling and traveling. Instead of moving on with the troupe tomorrow, he would ask if he could stay at the local monastery. Perhaps he would find out how to become a monk.

"You are welcome to stay here," said the Abbot, when Tristan went to see him the next day. "But you may not be suited to life as a monk. You're used to the freedom of travel and the applause of the crowd!

"The life of a monk is very strict. We spend much of the day in silent prayer and attend several chapel services each day. You will rarely leave the monastery grounds."

"But that's what I want!" pleaded Tristan. "I've wanted to serve God since I was a young boy. Surely being a monk is the best thing a person can do for God."

"Very well," said the Abbot. "I see your heart is set on this. Why not join our monastery as a novice? Then you will see how best to serve God."

It was not long before Tristan realized that the Abbot was right—it was going to be very hard to settle into life at the monastery!

He found it hard to wake up, so he was sometimes very late for chapel.

He found it impossible to remember the many chants they had to sing in chapel.

And he was certain the other monks prayed much grander prayers than he did.

"Listen to the Tumbler," whispered Brother Gervais to Brother Algernon. "He can't even remember a simple chant! He should have stayed where he was, cavorting about on village greens."

Brother Gervais and Brother Algernon liked to make fun of Tristan. They didn't realize that they were sometimes being really unkind.

Tristan could never remember when the monks were supposed to remain silent, so he often spoke at the wrong time. One breakfast time he wanted a hunk of bread. He remembered that the monks were not allowed to speak at mealtimes, so he caught Brother Gervais's eye and nodded toward the bread.

But Brother Gervais pretended not to understand. So Tristan tried again and again, but still Brother Gervais took no notice. In the end Tristan lost patience and spoke aloud, "Could you please pass the bread, Brother Gervais?" Everybody stared at him.

After breakfast, the Abbot told Tristan, "You must try to keep our rule of silence, or I may have to ask you to leave the monastery."

By now Tristan was feeling very unhappy. Life in the monastery was not what he wanted or had expected, and because of his bad leg, he had never gone to take food to the poor. Brother Gervais and Brother Algernon kept teasing Tristan, and he began to wonder whether God thought he was a failure, too.

The bell rang for chapel, but Tristan did not want to go. Instead he limped down to the crypt, sank to his knees, and prayed.

"Lord," he murmured, "I'm sorry I can't chant or say grand prayers like the other monks. All my life I've known only one thing—acrobatics! It's the only thing I've ever been good at. And now I can't even do that properly. Well, I'm going to try a routine now and it's not for other people to watch—it's just for you. It's the only prayer I know."

And, alone in the crypt, Tristan began to perform as best he could—walking in circles on his hands and turning simple somersaults.

Soon Tristan was missing every service to go down to the crypt and perform his routine. His leg was getting stronger, and for the first time in months he felt at peace.

But Brother Gervais and Brother Algernon had noticed Tristan's absence and wondered where he went. One day, they followed him all the way down to the crypt. There they hid in the shadows and watched in amazement as Tristan began to walk on his hands.

Tristan was enjoying himself, feeling he had never done more perfect somersaults, never leaped higher, never felt stronger. Then suddenly he began to feel dizzy and faint.

Tristan sank to the floor, feeling sick. Everything went black, and he did not notice Brother Algernon and Brother Gervais hurrying out of the crypt.

The two brothers went in search of the Abbot. They were sure that Tristan had exhausted himself tumbling when he should have been in chapel.

The Abbot looked sad when he heard their news. He knew that he would have to ask Tristan to leave the monastery because he had broken more rules. And he was worried that the tumbler might have hurt himself.

The Abbot followed the two monks down to the crypt. Tristan was still lying on the floor. But he was not alone—a figure knelt at his side.

Then suddenly, before their startled eyes, the figure disappeared! Tristan rose slowly to his feet. Unaware of the other monks, he began his routine again—performing perfect somersaults, turning elegant cartwheels, leaping high into the air, and landing firmly on the ground.

Awestruck, the other monks and the Abbot tiptoed away, wondering to each other, "Surely that was an *angel?*"

"Are you happy here, Tristan?" asked the Abbot the next day.

"No," said Tristan sadly. "I'm no good at praying and can never remember all the chants. And I wish I could help the poor like some of the other brothers."

"Well," said the Abbot, "I think everyone should ask themselves what they do best for God—and for you, Brother Tristan, that's tumbling."

Tristan shook his head sadly. "But tumbling isn't holy. It's not important to God."

Then the Abbot told Tristan about the stranger in the crypt. "Brother Gervais and Brother Algernon fetched me to help you. When I heard that you were missing our services, I wondered if you should leave the monastery. But then I saw the stranger with you. . . . I've never seen an angel in all my years as a monk, but that's what I think it was. I believe that angel was sent to help you and to show you—and me—that you have God's blessing to serve him as a tumbler."

Tristan suddenly realized he didn't need to pray wonderful prayers or memorize the chants correctly. For he had his own God-given talent—and, if he wanted to, he could use it to help others!

"You're right," he told the Abbot. "Tumbling is the best thing I can do for God. I'd like to leave the monastery and go back to life as a traveling tumbler."

"But before you leave," said the Abbot with a smile, "I would like you to give a tumbling display to the monks." And that's just what Tristan did. Leaping and turning and tumbling—leaving the monks wide-eyed in wonder.

The next day, Tristan left the monastery to become a traveling minstrel again. He performed alone, earning money as he went. When he had enough money, he bought food for the many poor people he met on his travels. And, when they had eaten, he entertained them by tumbling and walking on his hands.

And when they thanked him and clapped and cheered, Tristan knew that being a tumbler was important—because he was giving his best to God.